# I Love You Because I Love You

Written by **Mượn Thị Văn**    Illustrated by **Jessica Love**

First published in hardback in the USA by HarperCollins*Publishers* in 2022

First published in paperback in the United Kingdom by HarperCollins *Children's Books* in 2023

HarperCollins *Children's Books* is a division of HarperCollins*Publishers* Ltd

1 London Bridge Street

London SE1 9GF


www.harpercollins.co.uk


HarperCollins*Publishers*

1st Floor, Watermarque Building, Ringsend Road

Dublin 4, Ireland


Text copyright © Mượn Thị Văn 2022

Illustrations copyright © Jessica Love 2022

Cover design copyright © HarperCollins*Publishers* Ltd 2022

The artist used a brush, acrylic ink, watercolour, and gouache on Stonehenge "Faun" paper to create her illustrations.


ISBN 978-0-00-853165-2


Mượn Thị Văn and Jessica Love assert the moral right to be identified as the author and illustrator of the work respectively.

A CIP catalogue record for this title is available from the British Library.

Printed and bound in the UK

To my family.
– M.T.V.


To my mom & dad:
I love you.
– J.L.

I love you because . . .

because you're you.

I love you because you're here.

Because I love you, I am here.

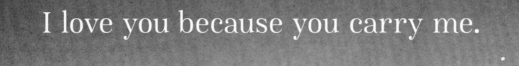

I love you because you carry me.

Because I love you, I am strong.

I love you because
you play with me.

Because I love you,
the world becomes
our playground.

I love you because you see what others miss.

*Because I love you, I see more than before.*

I love you because you let me speak.

*Because I love you,*
*love blooms where our voices meet.*

I love you because
you cook with care.

Because I love you,
food tastes better when shared.

I love you because
you let me make mistakes.

*Because I love you, no mistake is ever too great.*

I love you because
you know when I'm sad.

Because I love you,
I share the good with the bad.

I love you because
you're brave when I'm afraid.

Because I love you,
I am braver every day.

I love you because
you wait for me.

Because I love you, you're never too late.

I love you because you tell the best stories.

*Because I love you,
my best story is you.*

I love you because we go together.

Because I love you, we change and grow together.

I love you because . . .

because I love you.